THE CHALLENGE

and other Stories

My Journey with

Parkinson's Disease

when the body is the battlefield

Giulio Credazzi

"For my thoughts are not your thoughts, neither are your ways my ways, saith the Lord." Isaiah 55:8

giulio@credazzi.com
www.libro.it

Find it on:
www.Amazon.it
Paper - Kindle – eBook – Hard Cover

To my Friends,

Thanks for the great affection I receive every day and for the practical and even moral help given to me without hesitation.

Summary

Summary...9

Part I 13

Diary: years 1959-20XX 15

Introduction 21

2018 25

Foreign occupation..28

Siege 32

Throwing the ball 35

Ignored signals 36

Hurricane 38

4 January 2017 40

Handwriting shrinks 41

May the strength (that comes from outside) be with you...42

The neurologist explains 46

Nice ball!...47

Depression 48

Cold cane 49

When not selling the bike is an act of faith.............50

Non-Motor Symptoms 54

The Gondola...55

Extraterrestrial...59

Will 61

Water 63

It is not a transversal revenge 64

The toughest battle 66

Part II 69

TIME 71

Waiting for the starting gun 72

Brain damage 73

1973 75

Out of breath 78

57, 3 times 19 79

Time – March 1973 81

45 rpm singles 83

A stolen dream 84

Stillness 85

Dancing ribbons 86

The journey 87

The flame 88

The path 89

The friend who loves you 90

I'd like to kiss you 91

The oasis 92

Air: Hercules C130 93

Dedicated to those who died jumping 94

Everything's fine 95

Anguish 103

Flying 104

Youth 105

The lost friend 105

Breathing 106

The soul 108

The park 109

My Time 110

Sunset 112

To Ennio Morricone 113

Baricco and Leopardi's Infinite 115

My book 117

Lonely in London 119

My father 120

Pearl 122

Greedy 126

Comfortably numb 128

Computers 132

The missed embrace 137

McDonald's at Earl's Court, London 138

The Fourth Dimension 145

Part I

the CHALLENGE

Diary: years 1959-20XX

Although today the condition of Parkinson's Disease (PD) seems perpetual to me, it was not always so, for decades I knew no hospitals, no medication, not even aspirin or headaches, and a few injuries that disappeared as a child with "Vegetallumina" and as an adult with "Voltaren".

I always saw the more favourable side of life. I thought I would have my mother's life, as grandma or grandpa, lucid and long-lived. On my father's side, my grandfather died before I was born, my dad was 47 when he died, and my uncles died before 70. I never imagined that I would become a person 'sick' of a sneaky and complicated pathology to manage and live with, like PD.

I was born in 1959 in Rome, near Viale Medaglie d'Oro in Via Luigi Rizzo, and it seems I fell as a child because I found an X-ray dated 25 June 1959 and I was born on the 22nd - who knows what happened, could there be a connection? (with what?)

1960 my family moved to Talenti (North Rome) then it wasn't even marked on the map,

1965 I attended an elementary school called "Buenos Aires" and a primary school now called "Fucini".

1970 middle school at Barrili, which is now called "Angiolieri".

In 1973 just before the 3rd-grade exam, my father, Gianfranco, died of acute leukaemia, leaving an indelible mark on my small adolescent heart.

In high school, I went to the "14th" It is (tech institute), now called "Pacinotti",

I began my computer experience on "IBM" PCs, now called "Lenovo".

A concept I acquired while living this life is that everything changes.

I enrolled University in Engineering, but my mother immediately made me realize that there was no money to finance my studies.

I speak Italian, French, English and a smattering of Turkish.

I played football and tennis. I grew up in the Nomentano Tennis Club and reached a fair ranking in tennis. My first job was stringing racquets, and then I helped the club's instructors in the tennis school. Tennis went out the window when in

1980 I left as an officer in the Folgore. I didn't go for military service despite being asked to do so because when you're young. Your discharge comes in the summer, you hardly think about going for military service, and I felt that with the Cold War, there would be no more wars, even though there was no prospect of any job except that of tennis instructor.

1981 I retired with about twenty military and a handful of civilian launches.

After my experience in the Folgore, I emigrated to England to London to learn English. I keep jumping out of planes in Ashford. My first job was to be a waiter at the banquets of the Savoy because I only had to serve without speaking since I did not understand and hardly spoke English. In the meantime, Uncle Gustavo had a cousin who was a director of the BCI (Comit Bank), and he invited me to dinner to investigate what I was doing in London. My uncle was concerned that I didn't mess up, so I worked at Comit in Gresham Street, where I stayed for a good year, again because when you're young, you suppose to be smart. I didn't go to work in the foreign exchange room where I was supposed to end up from the accounts department where I was then.

The dealing room would have opened up new prospects for experience and earnings. Still, the proposal of a friend who manufactured and sold Italian furniture to mainly Arab customers in England seemed more attractive to me. I would have received a percentage on apparently large numbers and essentially zero earnings. This job turned out to be a flop, so after a few months through a temporary job centre, I returned to work in a bank, the Mitsui Bank, where I stayed for a few weeks. There was no talking to colleagues. I was monitored with video cameras in the room. Everything was in Japanese except the printouts I had to check, with zero chance of growth. I left Mitsui to join the Austrian Creditanstalt Bankverein, where I stayed until 1986. I got engaged to a beautiful girl from Rome for whom I returned, only to end the relationship after a short time.

I work in Rome as a freelance IT consultant. I work 15 hours a week and earn three and a half million monthly ITL. Thanks to the law that leaves all the VAT in the companies' pockets, I feel like I'm flying. I play tennis every day and return to a good level of play.

In 1989 I joined J.soft first as an employee and then as an agent. I got married and contributed to developing the professional software market in central-southern Italy for the company that, together with EIS, had the monopoly of the application software market. Microsoft offered me a job when there were still only 3 in Italy, and Windows was still at an experimental level. I refused to abandon the agency activity, which ceased in 1993, to start a technical-commercial business in the IT field.

In 1996 my daughter was born, a talented fantasy and comic book illustrator.

In 2007, together with other colleagues in the area, I founded the Trade Association, a group of 450 companies in northern Rome, anticipating the arrival of the business crisis,

in 2008 the book "from quota 33 to El Alamein" was published

in 2009 'Bible Prophecies' is published

in2013 we devise a strategy for eliminating public debt, which falls on deaf ears. If they had listened to us then, our deficit would now be 1400 billion, and Italy would have 200 billion in investment liquidity every year.

We create the newspaper 'Quadrante Nord Est', of which Uncle Gustavo is the director.

In 2013 I left home after being separated at home for years, and in

2014, after 40 years, I met again a girl I had dated at Circeo in the late 1970s, and a love story was born, for me, fantastic.

In 2015 the book 100 pages came out, a collection of 50 short stories. It is pretty successful, not at the level of "From Quota 33 to El Alamein", much appreciated, thanks to Facebook and Amazon by former Parà comrades. I have an accident with my Yamaha TDM 850. I break two metatarsals and the malleolus of my right foot.

2018 the beautiful Love story that began in 2013, and blossomed in 2014, ends as it began. Perhaps the onset of Parkinson's played a part. What I thought was a dream turned into a nightmare. To remember the period, I think it best to write her a collection of our letters, messages, reflections, poems and photos, of no less than 400 pages, the book I didn't publish is called 1799, the number of days in the story.

2019 I am diagnosed with Parkinson's disease. I follow the treatment of physical activity and Levodopa, but I struggle.

In 2020 I fell ill with COVID, so I was forced to stay at home in quarantine to edit "The Zollari", the story of my paternal family. After 21 days, the serological swab is negative, and we start again.

2021 I published 100 Pages edition 2022 and updated and republished "Silent Friend" 14 questions to God and his answers. In May, my sister died.

2022 I work on 3 books: "100 Pages ROME, The role of Rome in the context of Bible prophecies concerning Israel and the Nations".

"100 Pages The Power of Music". "The Challenge". I acquire the 'Gondola' device that facilitates walking for Parkinson's sufferers.

SUPPORT PARKINSON'S RESEARCH

PD
PLEASE NO DROP-SHOTS

Created by Eleonora Credazzi

Introduction

Here we tell, narrate, and describe emotions, sensations and experiences linked to a very disabling pathology that is quite widespread in Italy and the world, which in terms of characteristics and dynamics of its evolution, has many aspects in common with other neurological pathologies. Which now inexplicably affects younger and younger men and women.

It must be said that any severe and disabling pathology leads everyone affected to make the same argument; why me? Why now? What future awaits me? Is there a way out? How am I relating to others? Is my illness noticeable? Should I talk about it? Do I make others feel sorry for me? Does this physical problem stem from my pathology, or is it something that comes with age? Why do I feel ashamed?

Is it normal to be fatigued on five events in the third set? I am joking, of course, for those who have always played sports and set their lives with a strong sporting and competitive component, as in my case, face another frustration compared to everyday life; no longer being competitive at a competitive level.

So much so that I printed myself an ironic T-shirt about my handicap with which I invite people not to get bogged down in Padel.

Before I had Parkinson's Disease (PD), I was healthy. I took for granted many things in life that now seem insurmountable to me, which I simply don't feel like doing anymore, which are sometimes really difficult for me, such as getting up from my chair after a prolonged time.

I don't deny that I have sometimes thought of doing away with it to shorten the suffering, rest, and stop fighting. At the same time, I realize that every physical condition offers opportunities that must be grasped. They won't come looking for us.

These lines teach one to appreciate what one has. If taken correctly, they allow you to understand the gift of being healthy. In light of what I am experiencing, you will realize that it is vital to appreciate the fact that when you can run, swallow, eat at will, sleep and as much as you want, and even understand the importance of being able to turn around freely in bed.

I put ropes around the bed to get up and place my feet to optimize leverage.

Mine is not an invitation to enjoy myself concerning my misfortune. That would be a paradox, however, if my testimony can induce the reader to appreciate what he or she wants, attributing the correct value to life to the capacities and physical faculties he or she has, without having to experience something similar to mine, so much the better.

This is an excellent contribution to those around me and would be put to good use in a positive direction, which today appears to be a misfortune.

As my friend Riccardo from the sports club where I grew up says, 'I have become transparent for physical attraction. If we add the physical handicap for someone who grew up being told: 'you're as beautiful as the sun,' it is undoubtedly a hard blow to accept. I'll get over it.

The time has come to digest and metabolize this new human condition. As a believer born again in Christ on the distant 26/1/1983, even if today I cannot fully understand this 'gift' of the Lord, I know that the outcome will be positive in the end.

If I didn't understand it, I would say that the PD sanctions the fact that the best years are behind us. Moreover, I feel that life has always been characterized by the PD, like when we went to school, we only knew that condition, or still, under the military, we had the feeling that we had always been soldiers.

Life so far has been a sprint. I think of the things I've done, the fact that I didn't even take an aspirin, and I didn't know what hospitals were. Now I find myself over sixty with a young man's spirit, full of expectation despite a disease that I consider an accident on the road but which, in the end, was not meant to affect me.

There must be a mistake. I will come out of it in the end, as I always have. The knowledge of eternal life in Christ permeates every reflection in the existential sphere; therefore, every vicious mental circle that ensnares me towards depressive destinations eventually crumbles through faith.

The tenor of what I write is, at times, melancholic. It draws on sad or lonely states of mind. It does not want to oppress or be depressing because it is crucial to remember that all this is necessary to experience even emotionally real situations. For the writer, sadness is often the fuel that feeds the thoughts and pushes the pen to the paper, we must not be afraid of pain, loneliness, or sadness, but we use everything as a propellant to do things, to love, to act.

We could say that a sailing ship is like a narrative voice. With its open sails, it receives a gale-force wind that finds its strength in pain, sadness and suffering. Without this emotional thrust, the sailing ship remains stationary.

If the PD were a blast, there probably wouldn't be much to write about. Instead, it is a daily physical and mental struggle.

No one has ever been able to write that you can recover from PD.

I bought a nice pen.

2018

In 2016 and 2017, there were signs of slowing down movements, constipation, reduced sense of smell and fluency in executing automatic activities, and a constant and recurring backache.

I distinctly remember lying on the living room floor at home or in my partner's bedroom in London.

At times my thoughts were slowed down as if clouded. I remember a feeling of anguish, not justified, enveloping me, similar to the surface a baby might have when it feels the need to cry, a sense that I came to know much better later when the PD became full-blown. I got to know the feeling of dopamine deficiency.

- In July 2018, I was writing in my daily notes:

The new house is open. I get up in the morning and take a bath in the pool and then work, come back at lunchtime for a bath in the pool, then to the shop and have an evening bath again, even if it's late.

It's all charming and fun. I can easily play tennis and sometimes padel.

However, I don't understand why I have slowed down. I have the feeling of being drained and depressed. I seem to be running around in circles without achieving anything.

I sow but do not reap; I write good books but do not have a background. Evidently, what I write is good but not commercially worthwhile.

- In September 2018, I was writing:

I am afraid I have some ailment; my left-hand shakes, and I drag my left foot.

She is far away.

My back hurts, and I walk badly. I look like an old man, even though everyone compliments me on my fitness. I sow, but nothing grows, I play, but I don't win. I don't talk about Padel, where I often kick the crap out of opponents

If I didn't have eternal life, I don't know.

I sleep with Her; sleeping embraced helps me live and dream

- In November 2018, I wrote:

Lord, I pray that my physical activity will be able to rehabilitate me and regain normalcy of movement and how I walk; I pray that I do not have any severe pathology such as Parkinson's or a Stroke.

- Also, in November 2018:

Precisely on the 19th, during our last stay in London as fiancés, our relationship ended by 'her' will, which caused me great suffering at the most challenging time of my life.

Her last words sounded like an impatience at my slowing down with a not-so-subtle accusation that I had 'settled', i.e. settled for a comfortable situation.

Obviously, he had not understood anything, having probably assessed the situation superficially, and I think I, too, was quite confused, unable to fully comprehend the situation. When I think back on those days, they seem fleeting and foggy, similar to the falls where you find yourself on the ground without knowing how.

The closure of the relationship seemed sudden, final, irrevocable, almost an urge to run away from it.

- In December 2018, I wrote:

For now, I pray that I will not be distressed, for the end of the relationship has caused me immense sorrow, weighed down by indifference. I pray for my back, the slowness of movement, anxiety towards work, society in general and the future.

Four years later, as I write, so many days have passed, so many things have changed, so many difficulties have been faced, and I am still here, hopeful that something positive will happen.

If I had listened to the moods of these years, I would have been buried several times over.

Foreign occupation

You silently settle in, first the hand posture, then the somewhat dragging step. Every now and then, you engage in the 'robot mode'. It seems that you need more strength, more will, and more attention to make the movements.

I don't know if it's the medication or you, but sometimes strange sleepiness that I call 'heaviness' seems to come over you.

To go to the body and expel a marble, I have to make an effort as if it were a mountain. To put on a pair of trousers is like walking on a tightrope between two skyscrapers.

OK, we could say that taking it easy is better than being in a hurry, but sometimes the slow motion, compared to my pace, seems to go fast.

I couldn't clench my fist. This threw me into disorientation.

Ever since you arrived, all we have done is discuss. My mind does nothing but comment, evaluate, and quantify the impact of your presence in my daily life, and I tend to say that it is always your fault if something doesn't work as it used to.

Putting on my shoes with laces has become a feat. Maybe it's the 'belly', but having difficulty tying my shoes is depressing, as is getting up from my chair. I have to train by pumping like during the Military to strengthen my arms and lift myself from the chair.

'Sitting lion, standing prick' that's the reality for me. The other version is: 'Morning lion, evening prick' as the 'doping' effect diminishes for the day because, although I pay attention to it, food makes it difficult to absorb levodopa.

Gradually, each day the circle tightens, and simple and trivial things become a feat. Sometimes, it feels like you've put sandbags around my feet or a mason's sledgehammer nailed my feet to the floor.

Once I've started, I can't stop. I have to continue on my way, the path of the day, then in the evening, I just have to sit for five minutes, and my eyelids drop, and I fall asleep.

It sometimes happens that I get stuck, like sudden braking, losing my balance, or miscalculating the distance when lifting my foot, and so I hit the step, risking falling to the ground, as has happened a few times.

The condition of the Parkinson's sufferer is hybrid, especially at the beginning of the disease, the medication takes effect, and it is possible to carry out one's tasks and chores well or poorly in an almost usual manner.

As long as the 'fuel' prescribed by the doctor lasts with its effects.

As time passes, however, the drugs become addictive, forcing one to increase the doses and, thus, the side effects. This is why research into Parkinson's is of paramount importance because, in a few years, there will be many patients with ineffective treatments.

Disease is not the only enemy. We must take into account the role of the State, which through its wrongly educated officials, distant from reality, does not know the truth of what it means to proceed every day, having to fight for something normal for ordinary people. In many parts of Italy, they are, in fact, a broken reed on which those in a problematic condition try to lean, only to find themselves with a hole in their hand.

The Parkinson's patient can no longer perform the same tasks before he falls ill. He can no longer work the same number of hours at the same pace. He has to have time and economic availability to do motor therapy. Otherwise, he will be out of work within a few days.

This leads to a reduction in income and an increase in expenditure. If the Government avoids taking note of the situation and does not take responsibility for meeting the needs that have arisen with the disease, who will?

On the contrary, by failing to capitalize on the accumulated experience of the pathology at every opportunity, the commissions assessing the degree of invalidity trigger a tug-of-war that has nothing to do with the State's role for which the state exists. This position is decisive for the dignified survival of those affected by an irreversible degenerative pathology.

By now, the day is drawing close, and the sunset arrives, telling the spectacle of creation and life. Sometimes, when we are not distracted, it reminds us that 'life is a slice'. That is why it must be lived day by day. The Lord provides 'enough for each day's toil'.

beautiful as the Sun

Siege

Everything became more complex as the days went by, as if they were bandaging my body. Each day with one more layer, making it thicker, like a mummy, making any movement difficult.

Stepping down the stairs, accessing the car, climbing the steps, moving inside the house or walking.

Each day the body becomes more rigid as if it were an enemy that you have to fight against so that it does what you want it to do, even something as simple as walking or running ... 'running,' I laugh.

By now, my mind is full of thoughts about how to cope with this new situation.

But when I'm in the water or sitting, it doesn't seem to be anything different from what I was before. Then when I get out of the water or stand up and walk, I realize that there is a force inside my body that holds me back, makes movement difficult, makes me lose my balance and makes me slow.

I cannot get used to it. It is impossible to get used to it. Thoughts fly back to when I was normal, when I could roll on the ground and grass and compete in sports on equal terms. This premature old age is torture.

The mind is young, but the body does not respond.

I note that time is now short, and I fight a daily war that I may not win in the long run, but if victory is, it will be daily. Yes, today is my battle. Today I have to pull out my nails to do laboriously what I did yesterday with my eyes closed.

My mind flees tomorrow, avoiding projecting thoughts which would see suffering celebrated if they took shape.

My body may be defeated, but this reality probably allows me to drag many people to heaven. I sometimes cry and often see the emotion in the gaze of those who love me or simply have a sincere affection for me. The Scriptures would define mine as a heart of man'. I get angry a lot, and often, in fact, I get really pissed off, and yet, all this, at the end of the day, will bear good fruit to the glory of the Lord, I am sure. I don't know how; I don't know why. I have this privilege because it is a privilege to have eternal life and be a bearer of Christ's message of salvation.

This illness leads you to reflect a lot, to appreciate that you can still do something that, until recently, I would never have stopped to think about.

Throwing the ball

My competitive level in tennis is now nil, but the arm, as they say in the jargon, is always there.

Ivo, who has also been a club member for decades, says it was nice to watch me play when I was a boy. One loved to catch the movements and athletic gestures.

I also had excellent service, with a nice tight, angled ball, sometimes going out, other times to the centre, depending on the opponent's position.

I began to sense that something was not working perfectly when there was no longer the usual coordination in throwing the ball.

Each throw became a little dilemma, and the fear increased, lengthening the time with the opponents and the partner, in the case we were playing double.

I watched and waited for this throw that each time was too low, too far to the right, too far to the left, never high enough, and uncoordinated. With the bell-like movement of the service, in fact, I saw a slowdown in the activity of my left arm. The hand is weakened. I drag my leg. Something on my left side is disrupting the movement.

My attending physician sees that I am dragging my left foot and making me open and close my index finger and thumb as fast as possible. I can't even do that, he prescribes checks to rule out ischemia or similar things and a neurological examination, so in May 2019, I was diagnosed with Parkinson's disease.

The diagnosis is a cold shower. I start following the treatment of physical activity and Levodopa.

Ignored signals

I remember that well before 2018, I used to experience a certain slowness in my movements. For example, when I had to get dressed by pulling up my trousers and buttoning them to fasten my belt, I felt a particular difficulty that was not there before.

For example, when driving my scooter and stopping at traffic lights, I felt an uncomfortable sensation as if anguish was enveloping me that was not justified by anything.

When I played five-a-side football recently, I was often the target of teammates who did not spare me gleefully remarks about my speed in passing the ball, especially when under pressure.

As well as getting in and out of the car, I tired more easily while on the tennis court.

Selfie at Ashford

2 May 2019

Finally, on 2 May 2019, there is official knowledge that the thought hovered silently threatening when the step was short or had to be forced to lengthen to free itself from the disorderly proceeding.

The weakened and uncoordinated left hand sent a clear and decisive signal.

All this forms the diagnosis of something that, at first glance, becomes a nightmare, a bad dream that one hopes waking up will go away.

But I am already awake.

Sabaudia

Hurricane

And then the hurricane catches you by surprise, you have to leave the field, and you realize that the storm is inside you. The game continues regularly, and the teams, as usual, continue to propose their game, now in defence, now in attack. Still, you are outside a spectator and never called upon again. You have to take note that your time is over. Yet, you feel you want to play again, you think you can play, but your legs do not respond to Ed Sheeran singing "Shivers", and the rhythm of Maroon 5 with "Lovesick" is not enough to chase away the sadness for the premature farewell to the game of life. The game is still on, even if mine suddenly ends. For lack of strength, it saddens me to bid farewell to friends, and family, to leave you who love me.

Thoughts of bitterness dictate the direction to take to the emotions.

It's not over, though! "Better a live dog than a dead lion" (Ecclesiastes 9:4). Then simple music of Camila Cabello and Ed Sheeran's "Bam Bam" triggers like a switch on the track that would like to lead you to depression.

There is still much to be done for the Lord's work in this place. His presence in your thoughts makes all the difference in starting to fight inch by inch, muscle by muscle, tendon by tendon, without overdoing it, measuring your strength, because in a degenerative neurological situation, being without power opens the way to what damages cells.

After an initial moment of disorientation, daze, and confusion, I realized that drugs must be taken precisely

Daily new defeats characterise these days, such as walking and having to stop and lean against a railing, a low wall, or a bar. Inventing every now and then the combination of the lumbar belt with the postural corrector, asking an upholsterer friend to sew me pieces of Velcro and make splices to facilitate the 'fitting', to customise the pull of the straps as much as possible, to assume as straight a posture as possible.

When I keep my back straight by pulling my shoulders back, I play the bully, the Roman coquette, with typical phrases like: "did you look? Why did you look at me? What are you looking at? What are you, the real thing? No! Then the lead passes!"

4 January 2017

In a goliardic manner, my partner on this date sends me a vowel to tease me:
"Good morning. If you haven't noticed, we're walking along the river. However, I need you to lengthen the pace a bit because I must be home by ten o'clock, so we have to go a bit more berserk."

The path along the Thames

But the crux of this cute, seemingly neutral WhatsApp message reveals an attitude of my motor phase that I will later identify as something that stems from Parkinson's disease's development.

Handwriting shrinks

At the beginning of my PD, I had read that one of the consequences of the disease was that pen writing on paper would become compressed, so it did.

Since I was a boy, I wrote my reflections, meditations, and prayers, in notebooks using a pen. I still have dozens of notebooks, notepads, and diaries.

I always had a beautiful way of writing, linear, clear, and rounded. Now I don't understand how the words are compressed. The tiny letters are microscopic and challenging to decipher.

Yet I seem to be making the exact same movement, but the words that spring from the action are compressed, the letters piled up even though I am convinced that there is nothing different in the impulse that starts in the brain from that of a few years ago.

The consonants are flattened, the letters "n" and "m" are barely distinguishable, and the text hardly follows the horizontal line of the notebook.

Reflecting on the dynamics of writing, I realize that although I do not tremble, the brain travels much faster than the hand, and I am less synchronized. Thinking should slow down and wait until the needle has been written before formulating the next word.

May the strength (that comes from outside) be with you

Sometimes I feel that the energy within me to do things, whether manual or intellectual, does not belong to me.

While seemingly responding perfectly to commands, my hands seem far away from my shoulders, as if they were listless.

Similarly, my legs seem to keep me company. Still, they are little inclined to carry out their tasks, like getting out of the car, getting up from the chair, get out of bed. I have to make up my mind, place my feet in parallel, spaced out, well placed on the ground, slightly forward, then give myself a push with my arms upwards and begin the movement without sudden changes of direction, using leverage.

Photo: Piazza d'Armi Livorno jumping on the canvas 19 m angel slide

When I was an officer in the Folgore, we had to climb up the towers made of 'Innocenti' tubes, used for scaffolding when renovating buildings. On that occasion, they taught us to always have three points of support, two feet, one hand, two hands one foot, never one and one, and climb calmly and with awareness of movement. Now, this technique comes in handy for moving between tables and chairs, taking the stairs around the house, activities that used to be done with our eyes closed, and the so-called automatic and repetitive movements, which the lack of dopamine throws off.

Sometimes going through tight spots and bottlenecks, I have found myself pinned down as if I were drugged or drunk as if the body did not obey the commands. In fact, for a brief moment, I am like a stranger to the body, a kind of temporary hibernation in which I am the protagonist but, essentially, also a spectator, unable to easily change the situation.

Sometimes I stand still for a few minutes, waiting to be able to move. In essence, I study the points of leverage support. I usually move one foot and avoid stopping it but simultaneously tense the muscles of my arms and push with the forces of my legs, so the sum of all these levers gets the better of what appears to be paralysis.

It is no coincidence that one of the first names for PD was 'Agitated Paralysis'.

I am often reminded of the phrase attributed to Archimedes: "give me a foothold (or a lever), and I will lift the world."

After all, being a Para helps me do somersaults to relieve falls, a component now very familiar to my stage of pathology.

I find myself arguing with this body that I observe in all its clumsiness and slowness as if I had an outside eye. Sometimes, I make fun of myself. At other times anger explodes, I fill myself with swear words and imprecations, I insult myself, I sneer, and a solid Roman dialect emerges: *"m'anvedi come stai? Don't you see how you are? It takes you a quarter of an hour to walk two steps, to unscrew the cap of a bottle of water. It seems to me that you are unscrewing the spark plug of a motorbike! And then you don't even put your feet up, you walk on the grass, and it seems like you're going from one building to another with a rope. You were as cool as a kid as you are laughing today. In fact, you make me cry!"*

Every day is tiring. Every day I'd like to throw in the towel. Many friends call me brave, but I don't quite understand what they're referring to. I barely manage to do what I must to get through the day.

The neurologist explains

Parkinson's is a neurological disease, so the brain assumes abnormal behaviour, one of which is to convince me that I am weak, even though my muscle tone is the same. I do more gymnastics now than I did before I had this disease.

So when I have to make a movement that implies an effort, I have to consciously assess that the strength is actually there, so if I am blocked, especially with my feet, I change position. I move them, and in very close sequence, I make the movement that requires physical effort, such as getting up from a chair, bed or car.

Carrying this body around is tiring, and making paths requires a lot of energy, not to mention that I feel awkward. After a while, everything hurts, especially my back, because the position is not perfect. In fact, the department that treats me is called "Movement Disorder" when I am under stress, I feel my arms as if I have little strength, poor control of my hands, and my feet are heavy.

There's probably also something dopamine-related because sometimes I wait a bit, which normalises.

Nice ball!

One day we were playing mixed doubles with some friends. At one point, my opponent came out and said: "but he plays from a standstill and sends the ball where he wants. How does he do it?" His doubles partner indolently replied:" arm! It's called an arm! "

My lifeline that saves goats and cabbages is called "nice ball!"

When a ball arrives during the game for which I should make a dart, or it is a bunt, a distant ball, just exclaim: "nice ball!" and watch the ball pass, be it tennis or Padel and let it slip through, we give satisfaction to the opponent, and we have an alibi for the lost point.

Depression

In Parkinson's, depression is always lurking, much depends on the character and the ability to set goals and succeed in achieving them.

Undoubtedly the moments of solitude, in which silence prevails and prayer is suspended, the mind turns back and retraces the days that tell how the disease has insidiously taken control of the body, conditioning every moment and every aspect of life.

In those moments, depression can make its way in and occupy the little place left vacant by the PD.

One must assess the situation according to two factors: "Are you a believer in Christ or not?" If you are, you will know that He is in control of the situation and that everything cooperates for the good of those who love God, and if you face difficulties, they will never be greater than your ability to cope with them.

"If you are not a believer", your strength is negligible.

"If you are discouraged in the day of adversity, your strength is little." (Proverbs 24:10)

In both cases, the difficulties are the same, only the number and type of tools available to deal with them change.

Cold cane

The cold reed laid down reveals no flavour.

It is the day of abandonment

and of departure

the day wearily advances

the greeting is forgotten

the kiss is cancelled

the embrace dismissed

There will be no words to fill the void

From the eyelashes will flow the sad spring

The smile will not have its effect

Mourning will prevail over vanity

Your cold gaze will drive away the gloomy bite,

father of silence.

When not selling the bike is an act of faith

In just a few months, three years after the diagnosis, my physical situation had plummeted. By spring 2022, the Piaggio MP3 scooter had fallen on my left foot five times. The sixth time, it would have gone gangrenous. It took months for the abrasions on my left ankle to heal.

But I didn't sell the bike. I hope to recover in my heart, thanks partly to the 'Gondola', this medical device that accesses the central nervous system through the foot to support balance, freezing and walking.

As I write, these are days when my balance is very precarious. I get dizzy as soon as I get up from my chair after sitting for a while. If I stretch myself by helping myself with a column, a pole, or a wall, after having been bent forward for a long time, assuming a captocormic posture, it is not uncommon to crash to the ground, filling myself with bruises.

A few days ago, I lost my balance as I entered the house, I tried to hold on to the glass door, but it opened completely with my thrust, robbing me of my foothold and crashing to the ground, smashing one of the rectangular panes of glass in the door with my head.

The more days go by, the more careful I am to avoid falls.

One of the worst falls was from the steps behind the swimming pool, from which I fell deadweight onto my left shoulder, simply losing my balance by not having three points of support but only two.

I found myself in the dark alone for ten minutes, having hit my shoulder, elbow, left hand, left ring finger and middle finger on the concrete.

Being stronger than you

does not mean thinking that you do not exist, but ...

If I fall, I get back up
If I stumble, I pick myself up
If I lose my balance, I grab a stick
If you don't make me move, I play padel
If you throw my back down, I straighten it up
If you want to see me lie down as I lose myself in the ceiling, I dream
If you're going to petrify the expression on my face, I laugh.
If you push me from behind, I feed my lats.
If you pull me from the front, I nurture the abs.
And if the service ball doesn't go in, I tap from underneath.
You want me apathetic and tired. I will tell your story.
And if you would send me away, I feed on your smile.
And if you wanted to destroy my life, I would resist.
And if you want to blame God, I pray and thank him.
And if you would take away my hope, I celebrate life.
And if you would have me believe that life is over, I open the window of Eternity.

Non-Motor Symptoms
That May Precede the Typical Clinical Manifestation of Parkinson's Disease

- REM Sleep Behavioral Disorder
    (RBD -REM Behavior Disorders)

- Hyposmia (reduced sense of smell)

- Autonomic Dysfunction

- Constipation

- Orthostatic hypotension

- Depression

The Gondola

AMPS (Automated Mechanical Peripheral Stimulation) therapy delivered by the GONDOLA® medical device is an innovative, non-invasive and non-pharmacological approach that helps to improve motor disorders due to neurodegenerative diseases, such as Parkinson's and Parkinsonism, or resulting from cerebral strokes and ataxias.

The aim is to improve, in particular, gait and balance disorders, helping restore safety and speed to benefit the quality of life.

Clinical studies, with results published in international scientific journals, have shown that AMPS therapy improves movement by activating brain areas involved in its management. It also acts on balance problems and enables a reduction in the freezing of walking.

In most cases, the patient achieves positive effects on gait from the first stimulation during the fitness examination at a GONDOLA® Specialised Centre.

The benefits are generally felt two to five days after treatment, depending on the disease and the patient's response. Regular repetition of GONDOLA® stimulation allows them to be maintained over time. If treatment is discontinued, the effects gradually wear off.

AMPS therapy for Parkinson's, stroke and ataxias do not interfere with drug therapies or devices such as pacemakers or DBS (Deep Brain Stimulation). It is not a cure but a therapy to accompany the others, and the patient must continue to follow the instructions of the treating neurologist.

A healthy lifestyle and adequate exercise are the best way to manage Parkinson's disease.

Clinical studies have shown that exercise, supported by targeted rehabilitation therapies, can improve Parkinson's symptoms while slowing physical decline.

Parkinson's therapies are effective if they are consistent over time.

The progressive loss of motor skills can cause side effects: reduced movement leads to a progressive reduction in muscle tone and general condition; the progressive loss of autonomy can lead to loss of self-esteem and depressive phenomena; reduced balance and Parkinson's freezing problems cause falls.

In people with Parkinson's disease, physical rehabilitation is critical for maintaining good physical condition.

Among the rehabilitation therapies developed in recent years, the one that has recently received the most attention from physicians is AMPS therapy.

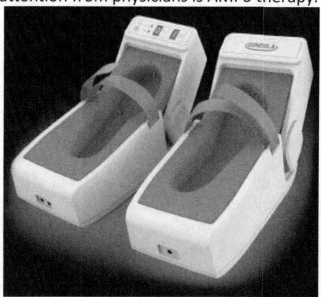

The Gondola must be said to be rather expensive, as the price is around 7,000 euros, and to receive its benefits, one must be able to use it as needed.

The way it works is effortless: you place your feet in the correct space on the insoles, press a button to set the heads of the device, and then press the same button again to perform the ninety-six-second routine.

This is the sequence:

Place the two Gondolas on the floor and attach the USB cable between them.

Insert the feet, remembering that the knees should form a ninety-degree angle, and there should be a gap of at least 30 cm between one Gondola and the other.

Press the blue button once and wait until the noise of the motors stops and the flashing LED turns steady.

Press the blue button once more when the LED stops flashing, and the therapy starts.

After ninety-six seconds, you will hear the sound of the motors coming back into alignment, and the Gondolas will turn off. Putting on your socks and shoes and getting up from your seat, taking two very long steps.

Then you are ready to walk, remembering that the first step will always be longer than all the others.

Very often, it happens that I move with great difficulty in the morning, so I make an application with the 'Gondola', and after about fifteen minutes, I feel my legs are lighter and 'lighter', with a 'slimmer' step.

The effect is not always long-lasting, but I understand that if I take the steps after the treatment more calmly and precisely, the more influential the result.

Q.   'I can do it every other day. In general, what are the contraindications to doing it more often?"

A.   "Absolutely, yes, there are no contraindications, although mornings are recommended, trying to keep to the schedule."

Extraterrestrial

When you suffer from a disease like Parkinson's, you are like an extraterrestrial because you cannot do many things that people around you can do easily.

You're different. You struggle to amble, to walk fast, you can't run, you can't eat all you want, every cluster of hours, you have to take Levodopa for the dopamine effect, you have to be careful not to overeat before, nor after.

You watch your feet to which you have sent a command that is not executed, and so you try to get around it by abruptly ordering your right foot: "move!"

And so you move forward to get behind the other foot and thus begin to walk. There are those moments when you say: I wish I were already home, but you have to stop, and you raise your arms along the pole on which you rest your back to stretch your muscles and your spine, and you see those who do sports moving with ease when you just imagining doing a pirouette go down long, to the ground.

The dynamics of the fall are elementary. All falls look alike. You feel stable and seemingly secure in your steps. All it takes is a clumsy movement, bumping into a piece of furniture or an object, or leaning on something unstable. You immediately start a run towards a point away from the place that a few moments before seemed safe. In a few fractions of a second, you calculate the minor damage and the appeal you need to grasp to recover your position. Slowness has gone out the window, and a whirlwind of thoughts ploughs through your mind while your eyes, like a high-definition scanner, map where you are, processing the grasping ability, distance, and consistency, of any support points or support.

The feeling is similar to when you have had a motorbike accident. You find yourself on the ground without even knowing how or why.

Will

It is strange that when you find yourself fighting a war that today they have said is lost because it was so for those before you, they have already fought it, losing it. You want to win it. Even if you find it harder to start fighting, it would be easier to think that you cannot do it. In reality, you have no choice. You must choose the daily goal, the hourly goal, or the goal of that instant, like getting up from your chair, getting out of bed or out of the car.

Pursue the goal until you reach it, without hesitation, without wasting your strength, measuring every aspect of your life, looking around you in the knowledge that you are different, not better but different, tired, weakened, worn out.

Then you try to understand what willpower is. You want to know how determination can be defined:

It is straightforward!

When you are sitting and looking at your feet, and you can't get up ... you stand still.

Everything around you, but also in your head, is running fast. However, you're standing still, waiting, you don't know what for, and you move your hands around, trying to find footholds for leverage to get up with as little effort as possible. Because your brain is saying, "I'm not giving you the energy to get up because I need it to breathe, I need it to pump blood with my heart, and so there's no way I'm going to give you the energy to get up and take a little walk." And you feel your feet like lead, fused with the floor, so you pull your foot back. You don't even let it stop in the end position. Then, you push with your arms on the armrests or the seat, discharging the thrust to the ground. And magically, your bottom rises, but be careful because that's when you fall.

So calm down, pause for a moment on the position and direction to take, and remember to stretch your neck and your back because the straighter you are, the less you fall and the less it hurts.

This is what happens on a physical and mental level when you see one of us getting up from a chair and going to get an object, a coffee or a glass of water.

Water

All pain and references to the PD disappear when I immerse myself in water. If I walk, I do it straight without effort, with no posture reminiscent of 'captocormia'. In other words, the position is naturally upright.

As you swim on your backstroke, you feel the water slide under your back, you feel as if you are flying, and you look up at the sky and confront God, who controls everything, even your illness. In fact, you know that he knows what could make you well, and in your heart, you invoke him so that the path to healing may be revealed to you. As you swim and float in the water, the aches and pains disappear, a sense of well-being envelops you, and you realize what your condition was like before the MdP.

Here is a cue for those who read and are in good health to reflect on this reality, considering that life can hold surprises, which in my case means the PD, getting familiar with the pains, and slow and complicated movements to perform. However, it used to be done automatically, with eyes closed.

Yet I am still the same, even though I sometimes feel I have always been in this condition.

However, something special happens as soon as I dive in, and I feel perfectly normal, like in the old days. On the other hand, a neurologist explained that the Parkinson's sufferer has no impairments or muscular damage. The brain shoots up a lot of nonsense regarding strength and motor capacity. Those with PD do motor rehabilitation to educate the brain to make movements. It is not post-traumatic rehabilitation.

It is not a transversal revenge

The psychologist asked me whether I thought this illness was divine punishment, so I pondered this possibility as a believer because I do not behave perfectly in God's eyes as a human being alive. Of course, one does not sin when dead.

Analyzing the pathology, it turns out that it began several years before his diagnosis. If it was something God had done, it would have begun well before when I deserved this condemnation.

God does not put intentions on trial. It does not work that way. On the contrary, I think that disease and all the evils of this earth exist as consequences of sin, as does death itself.

As far as I am concerned, I believe that although my disease is incurable or rather incurable to this day, I know God knows the answer to the condition. The cure is known to him. There is no reason why he should not reveal it to me, so I find myself with my ears open to what the Lord has to say to me about this disease.

He may not even reveal the cure, but I like to think so, and I want to. I don't know how, I don't know when, but in my life, I have seen that when He had something to tell me, He let me know, and I understood it.

On the other hand, this glimpse of life is at the Lord's disposal to be used in the best way possible to make the Gospel known to as many people as possible. So that they may believe and be saved, also thanks to this illness of mine. Perhaps by reading these lines.

If even one person is spared from eternal condemnation, this sacrifice will have been worth it.

On the other hand, the life that counts is not in this world but in the Lord's presence.

The toughest battle

All wars have different aspects and battlefields, with various elements, from guerrilla warfare to house-to-house raking, so the clash with the PD is crucial daily.

It is on a mental level. Where everything would seem to point to despondency, the real hard work that those with the PD do is to choose positive words, not blown up, to have a positive outlook on life, and to convey a positive message because this will come in handy for us too.

The war is won on this battlefield by learning to be patient, to accept and sometimes just wait for and respect our new limits because of our PD characteristics. If we can learn to live by this thought, this dynamic will keep us safe if and when our body gets worse, and the limits we have to accept are even more remarkable.

A good practice can also be to pray every day when waking up if there is one good thing I can do today.

I thank my family, especially friends, who often, when I meet them, especially after a long time, I see them barely hold back tears from emotion, recognising how effective this PD is in hounding me in my movements. I know it is like a punch from the bottom up to the pit of my stomach. I, too, I'm moved to see how much genuine and spontaneous affection there is towards me. May the Lord reward them. I know that some old friends, although helpful when needed, prefer not to meet me, so strong is the emotion at seeing the work of the PD.

We still have a card to play. I hope to write a new chapter with a victorious tenor soon... may the Lord assist us.

Part II

Other Stories before the CHALLENGE

TIME

Ticking away the moments that make up a dull day
Fritter and waste the hours in an off-hand way
Kicking around on a piece of ground in your home town
Waiting for someone or something to show you the
way
Tired of lying in the sunshine staying home to watch
the rain
You are young, and life is long, and there is time to kill
today
And then one day you find ten years have got behind
you
No one told you when to run; you missed the starting
gun

And you run, and you run to catch up with the sun, but
it's sinking
Racing around to come up behind you again
The sun is the same in a relative way, but you're older
Shorter of breath and one day closer to death
Every year is getting shorter, never seem to find the
time
Plans that either come to nought or half a page of
scribbled lines
Hanging on in quiet desperation is the English way
The time is gone, the song is over, thought I'd
something more to say

(Pink Floyd - The Dark Side of the Moon)

Waiting for the starting gun

You feel the energy you have that wants to live doesn't want to conform and wants to cry out to the world in anger with the things it sees. If you stop and think about it, you have to deal with that energy because you could choose and do something, but instead, you find that you are toeing the line and accepting the world you live in.

You see that the world goes on despite you, and you want to be in control.

But maybe it's easier to let yourself be carried by the current. Floating on your back, you close your eyes and let yourself be taken so you can gather your strength and understand how to deal with the force in you and the world around you. You are in the middle of it all, and you don't really know where to look, whether inside or outside, and you don't know how long you can look for and when you will actually have to do something.

You think that someone will come and show you the way, that you will receive a sign so you can follow your path, but it is only later that you realize that you've already been given a warning...

Brain damage

I needed to be crazy, to challenge fate when you didn't exist yet when I put everything I thought I had on the table. I looked for my own space, but I couldn't find it.
A pointless challenge that made me accelerate on my motorbike when I should have braked or lifted the front wheel instead of slowing down and challenging people who apparently never even existed.

That impatience pushed me to drive fast and aimlessly on the roads and through the sea, looking for someone or something outside of me while it was inside me, but I couldn't find it.

Feeling lonely and facing death took me far away and high up, yet I was running inside myself, and I might have done better if I'd kept still.

Looking for adrenalin by going out in the wind seemed to stifle all my pain, but it was only hidden; it went to sleep until the end of the jump.

You stop, and you think you're the one who's crazy because nothing goes the way you want it to. Maybe you don't even know what you want, and then you realize that your experiences are marked by the desires for things you don't have, and you're surrounded by too few smiles. Meanwhile, death looks at you, and you look at it so you can leave it behind you, driving towards it with the throttle wide open, trying to smother all the pain.

While your thoughts are sliding through your pen on paper, your soul calms down in the darkness. What was so restless begins to take shape and becomes a story that takes place in the present to comfort you in the day that is coming, if it comes.

Even though my soul rebels against the time it is living in, it doesn't need to run anymore or climb high up to feel alive. It hates everything in this world that is hateful and suffers with its islands of life and light.

My soul may sometimes go for a walk on the moon's dark side. It may well feel alone, it may actually be alone, and yet it's visible in this loneliness.
Loneliness is life's friend that walks with us along this path that makes it possible for you to look up and see what is alive and exists, beyond your eyes, that gives you the courage to put your hand on your face and be aware of life.

1973

A year that marked my existence forever. Death created a place in my mind that I had to deal with.
Conditioning my choices, moods, loves, friendships and challenges.

In 1973, Pink Floyd's record *"The Dark side of the Moon"* came out.
At that time, I didn't speak a word of English, so I didn't understand the lyrics at all. There was no Internet for finding the lyrics translated into Italian, like today.

But that was immediately special music for me and my generation of fifteen-year-olds. At home, "the stereo" was cutting-edge technology. My brother had made one-meter-high speakers with 30cm subwoofers and an amplifier with a one-hundred-watt RMS graphic equalizer, good enough for a discotheque.

After my father died, my nearby friends often came to my place, and we'd spend hours and hours listening to music. We'd listen to the same LP from the beginning to the end, even two or three times in the same afternoon, appreciating its nuances and stopping the record from listening to that magical bit again.

We'd sit on the floor in front of the speakers, on the rug or on chairs that just happened to be there, with the light off or very low, letting the melodies, the guitar solos, the piano or the drums penetrate deep into our minds.

We'd listen to everything from Deep Purple to Genesis, from Pink Floyd to Emerson Lake & Palmer. We listened to Neil Young, Cat Stevens, David Bowie, and many Italian singer-songwriters, including Battisti and de Andrè.

The Eagles and Creedence Clear Water Revival were always very special to us.

But the Dark side of the Moon has never faded away. It has been like a leitmotiv since 1973, the year it came into our lives.

The song 'Time' was always in the compilations of my compact cassettes. We listened to the Walkman or the car stereo.

Then in 1981, I moved to London, so I learned English, and the first result was that I could translate and fully understand all the songs' lyrics.

It was on those lonely, rainy days that I translated the whole Pink Floyd album "The Wall" since the film came out around that time.

Like Roger Waters said in an interview, I also had trouble watching life go on and thought I had to stand still and watch it without being part of it.
Because it goes on anyway, following its course, which you can influence or not, depending on your attitude.

Learning English and living in London opened up a

whole world for me. It opened up "the world," and I suddenly felt part of a global context, from England to the USA, Australia, South Africa and Canada.

I worked in an Austrian bank, and my colleagues were from China, India, Zimbabwe, New Zealand and obviously also from Ireland, Scotland and England.
I felt good in my new home. London had welcomed me well, the way you receive a grown-up, adult son, who has the house keys and his independence, and if he respects the rules for living together peacefully, he is free to do whatever he wants.

I felt I could relate to the Anglo-Saxon world just as much as to the Italian world.
The Tube, double-decker buses, big parks and gardens, cloudy skies, the rain and the joy when the sun came out, and even affection for the Queen, were all part of my new life.

Loneliness was a discreet presence, but I always felt it. Ironically that is my companion, even while walking along London's wet streets, looking at the front door doorposts with typically English, thick, shiny paint, sometimes white and sometimes an intense pastel colour. Black, enamelled railings with so many layers of paint that they were stuck. They didn't even close properly.

Out of breath

The train is rushing towards the station where you are supposed to get off; you don't know whether you want to get off or not. You think you can choose, but it's not like that. You look out the window at the ground zooming past without being able to distinguish the landscape or any details.

And yet all around you, everything is under control. Your feet seem to be firmly on the ground. If you want, you can go one way or another, but you feel the train is rushing towards that station. You want everything you feel in your heart to be in harmony with what is outside of you, but you don't even understand what the outside is. You just know that these are life threads and run along the rails. While moving, you're too busy with everything you are doing to know what to do to get off. You don't even know if you want to get off. That might be your very last stop.

You think you can identify a few details of the outside world and when you've got some idea, it's already changed, while you realize that you're shorter of breath and you know that at that speed you'll soon be at the station because every year goes by faster than the one before.

57, 3 times 19
(2016)

When I was in my first 19th year, I used to listen to "Time" by Pink Floyd from the album "The dark side of the Moon". I didn't understand the lyrics, but the notes spoke to me while I listened to it on my own, with the volume up high in the semi-darkness at home.

I'd run, and I'd run to catch up with the sun. Defiant and not caring about the time I had in front of me, I looked at those who were thirty as though they were just poor old people.
I wasted time and wasn't at all worried about its relentlessness, making fun of it by jumping out of aeroplanes that I raced to on my motorbike.

Then I understood this song's lyrics that describe life and time without God.
I could also relate to a dramatic, sincere song when the "next" 19 years came along, which flew away just like the music of a song while you are listening to it.

And now we're at the "third round", at three-quarters of the journey. There's no more jumping out of aeroplanes, and I go slowly on my bike to enjoy the ride. I don't know whether I missed the starting gun, and I don't know whether I should have waited for someone to say "go".

I've begun counting the days I have left, many of which I spend looking at my mother's face, just waiting.

I run away from thoughts of death now that I'm not challenging it anymore.
Maybe I'm more afraid of it now, even though I know my spirit is safe.

Every day, every month, every year gets shorter, I'm shorter of breath, and there doesn't seem to be enough time to fight like before to change the things that increasingly oppress me and everyone whose eyes are open.

What's left is that after all this? Like my " Time " musician friends, I have more to say and write about. Not imagining what tsunami is approaching.

Time – March 1973

Life is long, and I've got lots of time to kill today.
I think that sooner or later, someone or something will come and show me the way to go.

I see life taking its distance from my home every day. I watch helplessly as his life leaves him, he is talking to me, but his voice can't get through the air around him. He is fragile and is looking out of the French windows of the bedroom. Death has made an appointment with him and arrives on the 29th of April 1973.

For the first time in my life, I experience the prison cell of pain, the essence of bitterness and helplessness, and once you've felt that, it never leaves you again.

It comes back again while you look at the sunset and say goodbye to the person you love, waving as you walk away.
It hurts when you look at yourself in the mirror and realize how many years have passed.

You realize that more than 10 years have passed since you missed the starting gun, but you've run and run to catch up with the sun. You're shorter of breath and one day closer to death.

Every year has got shorter, and you never seem to have enough time.
You look at your smartphone, use it to get information, write on it, and read your thoughts and those of the rest of the world. You are in touch with so many

people, and you realize that many of them, especially your generation, have similar experiences and thoughts.

45 rpm singles

The record player's turntable automatically lets the single drop, while the arm with the needle at the end opens out in perfect sync to let it through.

The Beatles' music plays during the wet mornings of the 60s, and the English flavour of that music takes kids my age and older on a unique and extraordinary musical journey.

My brother wasn't even twenty, but he didn't have to do military service because he had British citizenship and a British passport. On the other hand, he had to renew his residence permit every now and then, which he had to carry on doing until 1973, when the United Kingdom became part of the European Union.

A stolen dream

You steal a dream from me.
You sink into a world where you feed on things that don't fill you.
I asked to walk for a short time along the path that occurs during the journey.

It would have been so easy if you'd opened your heart to see what your eyes could not see.

You imagine a field, and while you are looking, it becomes barren. After all, it is the field of loneliness and selfishness, which loves suffering because it thinks it feels alive that way, but actually, it's dead.

Stillness

And after the storm, I can hear the sweet sound of your voice, and I can stop and think about you.

I feel free to imagine that I'm close enough to feel you breathe and talk about this and that.

My warm friendship with you is there again. You are my oasis in a complex world.

I can't tell you how deep that feeling is. It's rooted in our friendship when we were kids. It wasn't essential then, but it seems to make sense of everything today.

I can imagine our hands and cheeks touching and almost smelling your perfume and feeling your skin.

The joy of feeling free to love you the way that only you know.

Dancing ribbons

At the foot of the mountain, the red ribbon lies lazily on the ground until a gust of wind picks it up and carries it lightly towards the blue sky.

For a brief moment, it meets the blue ribbon, and they play together, making beautiful shapes, and then they fly off in different directions.

The red ribbon flies to the "empire on which the sun never sets", and it embraces the bitter tree until it stops, maybe forever.

The blue ribbon flies high up and comes down without opening its eyes. Then it stops, thinking that this is where it will stay forever.

But that very same day, a strong wind picks up the resting ribbons, unaware of the journey they were about to start.

They rise up into the sky to a destination that has always existed, but they don't know it has something to do with them. Until the day they come back to embrace each other at the foot of the mountain. They have always been together, even before they knew the other existed. They belong to each other like a breath that needs air.

The air keeps the ribbons up. They are twirling around, making shapes that have never been seen, beautiful forms like the smile of someone in love.

The journey

I shut my eyes, and my mind starts its undisturbed journey. As I gradually get closer to you, I can smell your perfume and touch your skin. My body moves very slowly towards yours.

You're here next to me, I can feel your breath, and my body welcomes yours by letting you fit into it because it has always belonged to you, even though I only realize that today. You keep me company the way my thoughts do when I go for a walk on my own.

We walk together along the path drawn for us, experiencing something that cannot be bought.

The flame

I go ahead on my own on this earth, which is often sad and full of misunderstandings.

And even though I sometimes feel satisfied, something is usually missing. My thoughts float on an inner melancholic lake that keeps me company by nourishing my dreams and imagination, inspired by music.

Then a little flame gives everything a new light and colour because it wasn't there before. I never knew about it. I think this little flame is weak and bound to go out, but despite the strong wind, it doesn't. The light from the flame is reflected on the lake, giving it a warm, unique colour, and instead of going out, that blaze resists for weeks, months, and years and comforts me by nourishing my thoughts and making my path full of you.

The path

You fool around, you talk and say things you'll never remember, and every now and then, you kiss her. She comes up to you and then walks away again, or else you get lost while trying to follow non-existent directions. The rudder has been taken away, and the waves take you towards a harbour you think you've chosen, but it disappears as you get close to it, you weren't moving fast enough.

And yet she was the one that your heart was looking for. You didn't hear her voice, you didn't read her thoughts, you let her fly away from you, yes, because she does fly, she dances in the sky.

You've walked for ages with your thoughts and music without being afraid of finding only footprints behind you, and you're even far away from your own shadow since you're not following a path. Your heart is changed, and your eyes are open to see hers. You can listen to the voice and let words access the place inside you made for them.

You'd like to turn your feelings from your thoughts that breathe her into words to write down. You can only identify what they are when they talk to you. While your face brushes hers, the river flows, and your hand is in hers.

Words aren't even necessary.

The friend who loves you

Hi!
I'm the friend who loves you.
I've decided that *'I want the lot of what you've got.
And I want nothing that you're not.'* (U2 The origin of the species) I've made up my mind.
But it's not easy to put that into practice.
I'd like to sit with you in silence, look for a long time at those eyes that are looking at mine.
Kiss you gently, slowly. While I listen to you, I try to smell your perfume and touch your body, and my fingers are like a delicate comb running through your hair.
I'm the friend who loves you.
I've decided to keep you in my heart.
I have to learn to let you live
I have to learn to let you be
I have to learn to give you what you want at the right time
I'm the friend who loves you
I have to learn to like you, not to change
I have to learn to get to know you and understand you without upsetting you, without interfering.
How can I look at you without touching you?
How can I think about you without wanting you?
Hi!
I'm the friend who loves you.
Let yourself be loved.

I'd like to kiss you

More or less twenty kilometres across town to your
place, these days, I feel a kind of slow melancholy in
my state of permanent loneliness.
I sit down anywhere, your bedroom is cramped, and
many photos are on the wall.
I'd like to touch you.
I'd like to kiss you,
but instead, I settle for a kiss on your cheek when I get
there and leave.
I don't know what's going through your mind,
you're somewhere else,
you smile,
but you're distant,
impossible to reach on the path you are walking along,
which will take you far away from me.
This path is yours alone,
a way of joy and tears,
which will never cross mine.
I look at you as you walk around, talk, and joke with
that voice of a little girl. You have so much time ahead,
and life is waiting for you with its darkness and light.
I'd like to have kissed you, but it didn't happen.

The oasis

You walked a long way in the desert, with loneliness, cold nights, hot days, and no water.

What you thought might have been enough for you wasn't.

You wanted to die. It would have been easier to see no way out or future.

Everything was barren, dry, and meaningless, and you were tired and drained of all your energy. You had lost your willpower and were dragging your feet. You could hardly keep your eyes open.

One day you discovered an oasis with lush vegetation, plenty of water, and a cool breeze blowing through the palm trees; it made you feel alive again, and you knew that even when you had to leave it, you'd be able to go back there. That oasis reminds you that you're home, that it's the place where your heart feels whole, and finally, you know what life is all about.

Air: Hercules C130

I know you're there even though I can't see you.
I'm challenging you
You grab me the way a hurricane sweeps away a leaf.

You snatched me away from my shiny nest.
I'm looking at the shelter that is flying away from me
As I walk through the clouds

I can't hate you
Because you are all that is keeping me up.

And I'm alive.

Dedicated to those who died jumping

You shouldn't have come today.
You hit me like a swallow hits the walls of its cage.
The square jaw and the stern look have gone.

It didn't open. It betrayed me.

Salty drops wouldn't have stopped my soul from rising
and disappearing.
My drum stopped.
The path disappeared.
The water too.

Everything's fine

I look down my legs to my jumping boots that hold my ankles firmly. The laces are pulled tight, and my padded camouflage trousers are as familiar to me as a pair of underpants.

I've got my backpack with munitions for the practice drills, the K ration and some rocket parachute flares, very few actually for the whole company.

I have time to kill before I get on board, and I try not to notice my colleagues talking in the background.

The cargo door at the back of the Hercules C130 is open. I look at the anti-slip plates and the cylinders for loading and unloading supplies during the flight in inaccessible areas.

Once during our practice drills, we depended on airborne supplies for our food, but the boxes were intercepted before we got to them, and we had to kill some chickens so we'd have something to eat.

There are side rods to stop the cargo door from closing by mistake. It is simple and routine, like how mothers prepare lunch. The ropes are moved into position. Everything on the aircraft is made to the highest standard, using solid materials. The plane is extensive and impressive, and when they aren't moving, the propellers look as though they are warning you, and you stare, amazed at the number of fixing pins that lead to the gas turbine exhaust vents.

And yet it's so ordinary and familiar. It's part of me.

Time goes by slowly, and we're bored. Soon our feet will be on the aluminium of the door, and we will walk into the fuselage the way a football team walks into the changing rooms from the stadium.

Once inside, we look at all the aircraft parts fixed to the fuselage to optimize the available space and consider emergencies.
With their helmets, backpacks and weapons, the soldiers take their place on the tiny seats like the ones in the theatre when it is complete. There are no empty seats, nobody is left standing, and everything is planned perfectly.

I feel like I'm just going on an ordinary coach trip, but I'm taking part in a night-time tactical launch with a low-altitude route through the mountains across the forests of Tuscany and Emilia.

That's what life is like. Even something that, for some people who may appear to be exceptional, becomes ordinary in time. You get used to it, and your continuous search for something extraordinary can lead to a feeling of saturation, and you end up running unnecessary risks.
In the pointless race for intense sensations, you skip the details, the nuances that are what fill every experience with actual content.
This makes it possible to create that series of experiences, perfumes, and feelings that make up the depth of the human soul. They are all elements that make it possible to face life's adversities better.

The silent paratroopers sitting opposite each other on the rows of small seats look at each other uninterestedly, the way you look at people in the underground. Some people joke that they might not be back for dinner.

On the other hand, the operational units' soldiers, particularly the airborne ones, are described as " death's fiancés".

The lights are dim, it's dark outside, the engines are switched on, and they start making a constant noise that sounds like a jet. The fuselage doesn't vibrate much. It just takes a few minutes for the four large propellers to start turning. They speed up fast, the cargo door at the back that we came in through closes hermetically, and although the flight is at a low altitude, the fuselage is pressurized, like in airline flights.

The engines' vibrations and noise increase as the Hercules moves into position at the beginning of the takeoff runway. The propellers turn even faster, and the brakes are on and then suddenly released. The feeling is like being on a powerful motorbike when you open the throttle fully. The C130accelerates fast. You feel it much more than on an airline plane. It's as though it's got a turbo engine, a few dozen yards taxiing down the runway, and it's in the air.

After a few seconds of straight and stable flight, the aeroplane suddenly turns into the valleys of the Apennines, with the belly of the fuselage flying just a few dozen meters above the treetops. Then following the lay of the land, the aeroplane gains and loses height, just as it would if it were operating in enemy territory, to keep out of reach of the radars.

Inside everyone is bored and rather annoyed about not being able to sleep that night, and they are waiting for the signal that tells the first men to stand up. It's going to be a difficult night. First of all, you must find your bearings in the dark. And even though the point is indicated on the map, the reference points are confusing at night. So you have to walk a long way to find a safe place in the woods or fields, maybe an abandoned farmhouse, hopefully with not too many mice, where you can sleep until dawn.

It's time: twelve of us stand up quickly but calmly, without sudden movements. It takes a lot of effort because of the giant, heavy parachute on your back and the one for emergencies strapped onto your chest, with the backpack under it and the rifle or MG field machine gun at your side.

There's very little room, and keeping your balance is challenging, so you take small steps, walking in single file, six on one side and six on the other, towards the side doors open by now.
The change from the relative silence of the pressurized fuselage to the fury of the wind with the doors open in flight is staggering.
It's evident that the doors are open, nobody is surprised by that, we have to use them to get out of the aircraft, but actually, it's strange to see the door of an aeroplane open during the flight, even when you are just about to go through it to get out. It's as though

your thoughts aren't connected to the reality of your situation.

In fact, typically, when you travel, you see the flight crew lock the doors. Nobody could possibly imagine seeing one of them open during the flight.

You look along the edge of the door, see the red light, and you and the launch director look at each other for a moment. He moves confidently and reassuringly, showing with his gestures that he has the situation under control and everything is going according to protocol.

The air that fills the fuselage is cool and crisp. It has that intense smell that air has at a high altitude and makes a loud and constant noise. It's dark outside, and the lights look far away. It's like looking at the panorama from the top of a mountain. You feel the adrenalin. The loud noise takes you back to when you were a kid and how much fun it was to make a lot of noise without anyone complaining.

As a soldier, you can make a lot of noise. The aircraft and the helicopter turbines are noisy, the noise the tanks make when they go past sounds like a herd of horses galloping by, and hand grenades, rifles, bazookas, mortars and cannons all make plenty of noise too.

When you're making the noise, you think you're the master of the world, but if the others are making a lot of noise (and you can't do anything about it), it's not fun. That's what used to happen on the first days at the officers' training school, when at three in the morning, while you were fast asleep, the elite troops from the other course rushed into the dormitories, switched on the lights, hitting the sides of the bed or the metal lockers. They threw the windows open onto the cold night of the Cesano countryside. They kicked us out of bed and made us clean the dormitory, the corridors and the bathrooms yet again, even though we'd only just finished it all at midnight, with a final check for dust with a leather glove, usually under the feet of the bed or on the window sill.

Military life is full of loud noises; the bugle sounding to muster the troops/ranks or to salute a fallen colleague, the troops marching and singing, and the noise of the column moving forwards. These are all specific sounds and noises that characterize the phases of military life that you remember forever, just like the feeling you have when standing a few centimetres from the open door on the side of the fuselage of the Hercules C130. It's a feeling you'd like to have for a long time. You're not in a hurry, you're not worried about it, and there's no specific time when you must go. When you feel ready, you'd like to push off into the void, but the pilot is concentrating on getting onto the trajectory for the launch and calculating the point when he'll give the LD the six seconds to launch and then switch on the green light.

The LD takes you to the edge of the door, your hands are half outside the aircraft, your legs are slightly bent with your right foot in front, and your toes outside the aeroplane, your left foot further back inside, like at the start of a running race and your whole body is tense and braced, ready for the signal to go. These are precious seconds that make a person strong and courageous. The wind blows at three hundred kilometres an hour and lashes against your face like a rough, scratchy piece of cloth.

At that point, you do not think you might die. You're only focused on repeatedly following the protocol you've been through during your training and in action. You ensure you see and hear the orders so you can carry them out promptly, without hesitating, and without thinking about anything else. You stare at the red light next to the door.

You hold your breath, almost as though you could stop time like that. If you could, you'd stop everything around you to fully appreciate that moment of your life that you will remember forever because you feel that it's something that is part of you. This is something purely personal that nobody can contaminate. These moments seem to be suspended in the universe, as though you'd been able to create a dimension that fits perfectly into life.

Outside, it's pitch dark, and the air rushes violently from the open doors opposite each other. The hands are outside, arms are stretched out, and your weight is toward the back, like jumping over a ditch. The light turns green, and the LD gives you the signal. You must push hard to go because the wind is furious, but once you have jumped, it grabs you like a fast-flowing river. It tears you away brutally from the aircraft and pulls hard at the rope, ripping the parachute open.

Another specific piece of the puzzle has found its place

among your experiences, and even though the world will never be able to understand what you're doing, these moments make you strong. These are when you are on your own, and you stop for a moment in silence to look at where the sky meets the sea, and you try to remember that intense experience. The wind at that moment reminds you of the air rushing into the aircraft and lashing against your face. These feelings are strong enough to turn an ordinary young Italian guy into a parachutist of the Fifth El Alamein Paratroopers battalion of the Folgore Brigade for life.

Anguish

The confusion carried by the gust of wind grips you
suddenly in your deepest thoughts or comes to you on
the notes of some music closing the base of your
throat.
And you feel out of breath,
and you don't want to talk.
The streets are unfamiliar,
you're alone,
completely, intimately,
consciously, alone.

A well-known state of mind,
experienced many times, not bound by circumstances
but living in you,
often asleep,
that wakes up again at dawn in a Greek port
waiting for the evening ferry,
for a destination that takes you far away from your
heart,
while you watch the morning waves
broken by the north-east wind,
and you realize that you are alone,
and you smell the sea air.
You feel lost and wrapped in that feeling, as though it's
your whole life. These feel like sad moments, but
actually, they are moments of the essence of life, of
the breath that disappears,
That may only stop at times like this, so you can get to
know and appreciate it.
Yes, maybe the moments of anguish are the ones that
tell you what life is all about.

Flying

Alone,
among the white mountain tops
following your thoughts,
spinning along unmarked paths
that dissolve behind you.

The cold air is more comforting than punishing.

Adrenalin fills your chest and
you love the risk.
You think this is the path and that loneliness won't
leave you.

A wing brushes by you,
A breath envelops you
while your eyes meet hers, and you start the dance.
Words aren't necessary,
thoughts are more gratifying than physical contact
her lives in the deepest part of your breath,
the mark is clear and lingers on,
you know you won't always fly,
you let yourself be carried by the current that takes
you
on this flight

while she looks at you
and you feel alive.

Youth

You, the wind of the Sultan that shakes the leaves in
the silence of a hot afternoon,
you inspire my thoughts about life and hope.

Great is the value of the few days that have elapsed

Wonderful are the dreams
that sail on the waves of time

The golden halo wraps the gaze that blossoms from
the young branch

The lost friend

Dear friend flying past, shaken by the swirling air
Your race will soon be over
You'll know that there is no beyond
The current stole your breath

It closed your eyes

The race is over

There's no salvation

The wave took your mark away.

Breathing

And you feel the moments ticking away.
And yet once, a long time ago, you were the one doing
the chasing,
scornful of the risks and the danger, you made fun of
death, you came close to it, ran around it,
full of life, with that sarcastic expression and the
confidence that only immortal beings have.

But your breath is the same as before while the sun
approaches the horizon
And you can hear your voice, your words,
come from the kids who greet you formally.

Even though you feel that you're not far from it,
you know that death is breathing down your neck but
not down their neck, or at least that's what they think
like you thought when
while you were flying,
you stared at it and laughed defiantly.

And you look at the features of her face that are just
like yours,
and you know that her spirit is alive behind those eyes
that are your eyes.
Still, everything else is tired and wants to go away
because it knows that the sun has gone down under
the horizon, and you look at those small steps taken
with such a great effort. Everything is difficult now,
even lifting her arm to get a plate.

Spending her days waiting for that breath to become a

touch at the end of the path that began when the sun
was high in the sky and the day seemed to be infinitely
long,
whereas all that is infinite is that silent, discreet
breath, never worn out, only therein silence and
loneliness.

That part of you that is unique and knows you through
and through and talks to God,
that gets excited about the music that touches your
soul
Or a few lines you wrote when someone lent you a
pencil.

While the sun doesn't seem to want to hide anymore,
you wonder if there's anything left or if it was worth it,
you look at the faces in the photos on the table of
those who are waiting for her,
who you often think of or say something to without
receiving an answer
in the slow wait for that touch that brings us all
together.

To my mother

The soul

It's not easy to get to you.
It takes quiet, silence,
peace.
You're very sensitive
, and you don't like noise.
Being able to see you involves some preparation, a
rite, rules, and a specific type of behaviour
, and if I don't respect this, it's simply impossible to
find you or get close to you.
I approach you discretely
 and politely,
looking for what the world calls harmony.
It's not easy to get to you,
There are a lot of ropes that hold me back and keep
me away; sometimes, it takes a lot of strength to be
able to carry on walking towards you.
Then suddenly, you start talking,
I feel your breath run through my body, showing me
the part of life that I know exists,
but that is so difficult to get to know and touch,
that I only completely understand
when I listen to you, I stop and think
and that lets me appreciate a piece of music, thoughts,
words, and emotions expressed by other people I
know.

The park

The park is empty, and my dog is running around near me,
the grass has been cut,
the air is hot,
it's alright under the trees. I wouldn't say that it's cool,
but walking there is pleasant,
I amble, just fast enough to keep moving.

As I walk on, I think that this feeling that this is all that life is about giving me a subtle sense of lonely bitterness, with just a little sweet, resigned anguish, which by now accompanies my every moment of lonely reflection.

And yet when I look up at the sky filled with that powerful summer sun, I realize that I won't always feel like that, even though I don't know how this is possible. Now I know it was true.

My Time

Loneliness doesn't have friends., As time goes by, my time and my thoughts fuel feelings that cannot be shared. They can only be breathed. Maybe later, I'll be able to think about trying to understand them if I want to understand them if I'm interested in understanding them.

You die alone, you look up at the sky alone, and you breathe deeply on your own.
And while I look at the sun over my sea, a tear comes down, and I know that I'm witnessing the last greeting of the soul.

Who knows the depth of that emotion that only creation knows how to elicit from a quiet voice and heart? In the silence of your thoughts, fuelled by gazing at the horizon where the sky meets the sea, and if it weren't for the sinking sun, I wouldn't know where one begins and the other ends.

These emotions make life what it is, allowing you to understand that it is worth being human.

Time is not short, and not long either, and actually, I don't know how to suggest you spend it.

But one thing I can undoubtedly say is this: if you happen to be able to love someone, don't be afraid to love her!
Love with your whole being, don't be afraid you may be wrong and don't be scared of being betrayed,

cheated on or not loved in return. Let yourself experience that emotion fully, even if you know it will be a memory as soon as it is past.

Let go and think about her. Life has too few beautiful things to let something so beautiful and real escape.
When you're with her, caress her, run your fingers slowly along every tiny part of her relaxed body, brush your lips over her from the top of her head to the tip of her toes and then you'll be able to imagine that you really did it.

If you write it down, you'll be able to give it shape, and that feeling of pleasure, love and complicity will be able to live again in your thoughts, keeping alive the part of you that loves and that can be loved.

Sunset

The sun sinks slowly into the sea.

My strength has left me, and the world has lost its charm, my scars no longer tell their story, but behind my eyes, my soul is the same as ever. Thinking about my life, only one thought is still alive: I loved, without reservations, letting go of my soul and my feelings, managing to breathe your body, your eyes, your mouth, your hands.

I wasn't afraid of being betrayed or abandoned. I wanted to experience this love as I'd never have been able to imagine it could be.
The sun disappears on the horizon. It's time to go. It's time to leave this beach, my lips are salty, and my throat is tight. It's time to go, but you will always be there, and what I feel for you has marked these sheets of paper forever, and nobody will be able to erase it.

Today is over, the sun's gone down, and my breath has stopped, but what we are will never end. What exists can no longer not exist.

I recognise love in her eyes as if they are alive in me. I know I loved her if I closed my eyes and saw hers.
It's time to go. Your lips are salty, but I know I haven't lived in vain because I've known true love, the emotions that it's worth living for.
Behind my eyes, there's the same guy as always, but it's time to go.
And I still love you today.

To Ennio Morricone

Sorry if I'm informal with you, but you know what we Romans are like,
even if we don't know each other, you, with your music, are in my heart.
So on this 6th of January,
with this cold wind blowing hard from the Tiburtina mountains,
that hits me on the back of my head while I'm sitting on this bench
so the dogs can sniff around in San Basilio park,
your music's as loud as loud can be in my headphones.
I'm thinking about the day in the end, and don't tell me you don't think about that too, I think about it, and I'm practically only half your age.
But I want to be sure that when it's my turn,
you'll be up there, too, because spending eternity without your music would be a pain in the neck.
Life and death are serious matters, and we can't play around with that.
You won't know this, but as far as I'm concerned, your music is sung and played by angels, and it gives you that feeling that when you look up at the sky, you remember we've got a God that created the sky and earth, the sea and the mountains, the sun and the moon, and gave us a soul that never dies!
'Cos when God does something, it never ends, and something that exists can no longer not exist!
And I want to be sure that your soul always stays with the Lord, who died for us to give us eternal life for free.
I've got this eternal life, and I don't care about dying, and I want to be sure that you'll get it too.

That's why I bothered writing this, and I hope it gives you a little comfort, hope and serenity, even though it's nothing compared to what you've given me and the whole world with your music.

Thanks, Ennio

NB:

The music that inspired this chapter is: "The ecstasy of gold."

https://youtu.be/IE8YOvuhIcQ

Baricco and Leopardi's Infinite

The Infinite

I was always fond of this secluded hill
and this hedge which hides from my view
so large a portion of the farthest horizon.
But sitting and musing here, I picture to myself
interminable spaces beyond the fence,
silences beyond the human grasp,
and stillness so profound
that my heart is almost frightened.
But the moment I hear the wind
rustle through these leaves,
I compare that sound with infinite silence,
and I call to mind the eternal,
the dead seasons and the present
alive with all its turmoil.
In such immensity, my thought is drowned,
and it's pleasant to be shipwrecked in this sea.

G.Leopardi Translated by G.Singh

You seem shy, almost uneasy or embarrassed. Maybe
you're afraid that you won't be able to convey the
great things you have inside you to the people listening
to you.
Like a torch in the darkness of a room that you know
well, it lights the way and the objects in it to explain
and describe them with words to simultaneously make
them unique and familiar.
So your explanations gracefully guide us so we can
appreciate aspects that appear ordinary or proper

under your nose, but you can't see them.
Like "The Infinite" that you are about to recite. Taking your time, following a rhythm that is unknown to the lifestyle of our times.

And step by step, we walk into a world with a unique atmosphere that delicately balances the harmony between our thoughts and our soul., These moments create a vibrant space and atmosphere, which is what you acquire when you manage to appreciate what you already have.

Like being Italian. Letting us understand how privileged we are to be able to read things that belong to us in our own language and learn to see the aspects of them that no translation could convey.

Thank you, Alessandro

My book

Sometimes I see you as a shelter, somewhere I can go to listen.

When I find the subject that fills the pages, I feel something "warm" and comforting, like coming into a mountain chalet from the cold for a cup of hot chocolate.

You compare and develop your thoughts. Your ideas follow each other, and sometimes you have so many that you have to stop and write down an idea or a view that you feel is beautiful, relevant or interesting because you know that if you don't, it'll disappear.

You know how to start, but you'll never know what the end will be like until you finish and make it final. You probably won't reread it, at least not for a long time. You read it and reread it so often before it was printed.

As for journeys, what's important is the journey itself, not the destination.

And if we thought about life the same way, everything would be more straightforward.

The destination is death when you reach the last full stop and everything finishes.

Up to that point, we write our pages, which may be tired, repetitive, and full of joy or suffering, and our journey is told and set in time.

And every journey is like a new life, which doesn't overlap or conceal the previous one. It is a deep, authentic, less disturbed, not less troubled life that follows the path that we have decided, even though its pages talk to us and influence us and sometimes condition the choices in this life that are taking shape on our sheets of paper, which is no less ours than our everyday life.

Lonely in London

Coal-fuelled central heating must have still been widely used at the beginning of the '80s. Goods on display outside the shops in Angel had a layer of black spots that showed up even more when it snowed.

In winter, the sun has trouble rising, and when it's out, it stays pale rather than tepid. I'd say, in terms of the temperature, that it's irrelevant.

In our life, we are alone. The sooner you realize it and get used to it, the better you will live. But when you emigrate to a place where they speak a different language, which at first is impossible to understand, the feeling of loneliness is absolute, complete, total, impenetrable, and stays with you for a long time, despite whatever human contact there may be.

I walk along roads, through parks and down avenues, watched by that yellow-orange eye that dominates the silent sky. The Beatles' music from "A Day in the Life" seems to be the perfect soundtrack for this atmosphere with its humus for growth, allowing inspiration to appear among the fears, desires, fantasies and boredom.

My father

Inspired by the song "Sometimes you can't make it on your own" by U2.

A little boy with big dark eyes and long eyelashes,
he's thirteen, but he looks younger.

Life has shot him in the heart, but he doesn't know,
he can only feel excruciating, stabbing pain,
that penetrates deep into the most hidden and silent corners of his little being,
that annihilates his tears.

He keeps still,
he's motionless,
someone much taller than him is in front of him, looking at him,
he has something to tell him,
but he doesn't want to say it.

Suddenly his house isn't home anymore,
but a sad, empty building,
the world is a desolate, meaningless place.
The others are "just noise",
they're not people anymore.

A frighteningly powerful but particularly quiet hurricane,
took away everything he had.
Even things he didn't know he had.

His heart was broken,

maybe that's normal,
But it was broken.

People say I look like my father,
I look at myself in the mirror, and now I'm the same
age he was when he died,
I stared at myself as though I was saying:
 "You left me alone. I told you, please don't leave me
alone, without you, in this wicked land".

I'd have wanted to fight here with you,
maybe we'd have argued, and perhaps I'd have taken
some of the punches for you,
you'd have taught me lots of things I never learnt,
and maybe I'd have made a lot fewer mistakes.
Sometimes I don't think I can make it on my own,
I'd have wanted to be able to say:
"don't leave me here, yes, here, alone."

Pearl

It's been pouring out there for two days now, and the tent is soaked. Some drops of water are seeping through it even though the ropes are pulled as tight as possible, and its sides are perfectly smooth.

There's mud everywhere. There was grass growing on this field, but that's just a memory. There's no way out. The hills around us are in the hands of the "Rouges". We haven't had any supplies for days. They are dropped over our enemies. So all we have in terms of equipment and ammunition is what is left. I don't think many of us will get home. The vegetation surrounding us seems to besiege us even more than our enemy. Maybe it's a good idea to think about these last few moments of life that the Creator is granting us. We've seen too many comrades die by now to believe we can succeed in this business of staying alive.

Tomorrow we will attack to create a bridgehead that will allow us to escape. Still, the enemy is too strong. It's a solution only because there is no natural alternative except suicide, and we're nearly at that point anyway. Still, it's always better than dying in a prison where you're put in a cage immersed in water, where you have to stand with just your head sticking out so you can breathe, full of mosquitoes, with rats running over your hands that are holding onto the canes that close the top of the cage.

Life tastes bitter today. The hopes and enthusiasm in doing something beautiful or exciting on this earth drown in reality, like your bare feet, which, when you get out of the camp bed, are covered in the tepid mud that has flooded the tent.

I think of my pearl, which I won't ever be able to see again. Today it would be enough for me to live one more day with her, just one day of joy that would last my whole life, and let my mind be absorbed by her. It would be enough to touch her hand. Because there's something great for us made of strength. I didn't believe I had it or even thought it existed. That lives in my chest and cannot express itself now because there is a minefield around me. Pearl is on the other side of the enemy's wall.

So many couples in the world can love each other freely, experience that special feeling of sleeping in each other's arms and wake up with the joy of being close to each other. Being able to look into each other's eyes freely, knowing that the person you're looking at is someone special, unique, that they know you and love you, the only one out of seven billion people in the world. Still, you let the essence of your relationship drown in your ordinary routine life, household chores, and money problems, the same way the mud in the tent has reached your ankles.

But today is more than likely the last day of your life. It was destiny for the others who tried the same mission but didn't return. They never even reached their destination.

I don't want to die without embracing my pearl again

and holding tight for a long time in my tattooed arms, not without telling her that I love her and that having met her has given my life meaning. She showed me what true feelings come from feeling really loved, in a simple way, naturally, almost unwittingly, as though it were something that's not hers, but that comes from above.

Knowing I'm someone special to her makes me even sadder because I have to leave her in this land of wolves. Who's going to protect her? Who's going to stop her from feeling lonely anymore? But she'll never be alone again because she has a unique, authentic relationship that cannot be erased, one of those things that only rarely come about on the earth, that can survive the events of life and even death.

One of those relationships shows that God exists, but He abandoned me in a mud pool surrounded by mines and enemies for some reason. I don't want to argue with Him. The argument wouldn't be fair. Maybe this is the only way I'd have really learned how great He is and understand that "what is essential is invisible to the human eye".

I have to organize my company's escape. We have to move through the minefield behind the enemy lines.
We must break the siege and get reinforcements, that is, after hours of walking, being concerned about stepping on a mine or being ambushed.
The goal may be nearby, but there are still plenty of pitfalls. We have to move very carefully and watch out for traps, and even though we are almost safe, the

area is in the hands of the enemy.

I feel something like a splinter in me, I look around, but I can't see anything unusual. My legs won't keep me up, and my body doesn't respond to my brain's orders. Everything goes dark, and my body falls to the ground like a sack of potatoes.

My pearl is standing next to the body lying there, tears streaming down her beautiful face. She feels as though her stomach has been gripped by a steel hand. As a child, she'd never have thought she'd have to go through such a dramatic and intense experience. She'd never have thought that she could feel anything like that. Not letting love from emerging freely.

But then, one day, from inside, love suddenly bloomed and overwhelmed her, making her cry with joy, maybe secretly, but happy to have found real hope, being sure of the existence of a true, authentic, indestructible feeling reinforced by an unbreakable bond.

Her loved one's eyes are shut. The beloved lies motionless in front of her. Was it worth loving? She wonders. Of course, her heart answers. Some people don't know and will never know the meaning of that feeling. That overwhelms everything in your body and mind, a feeling that, for those who have never experienced it, even for a minute, would be worth a lifetime compared to nothing.

Maybe he will open his eyes, maybe not. What's important is to have really loved each other.

Greedy

You don't like publicity or fame. If you could avoid it, you wouldn't even be included among those who exist, but at the same time, you're satisfied with the power you think you have and the person you think you are.

You haven't got a well-known name. I can't call you by your name or identify you. You escape. Your soul wanders around the earth, unable to understand its essence, suffocated by everything you stuff yourself with, making your neighbour the cause of your terror. You don't even trust your own shadow because you never know when enough is enough.

Is it ever enough?

Is there anything that looks even vaguely like a limit?

Greed equals infinity multiplied by minus one. It's the opposite of "enough". If you're Greedy, you'll never be satisfied. You're a slave of what you don't have, unable to enjoy what you've forgotten, that is, what you already have.

Until the day when you'll be carried on people's shoulders, everything you wanted and got throughout your life will only produce conflict and bad feelings among your successors.

You've created a closed circuit system, which gets richer and richer on what it buys but has no value by cutting itself away from the real soul of the world, of people who may well be worried. Still, they breathe real life, which you'll never know because you live in fear, fear of your neighbour, fear of losing what you think you have, and fear of dying.

You have more than you could spend in ten, a hundred or a thousand lives, but you still don't stop. You impose suffering, and sacrifice, following a logic, yours, that looks more like drugs than thought.

You're that father of the seed that generates hate.

Your love for what will never love has consumed your greedy soul that still wants what you won't be able to take with you. Maybe you'll be moved when you're surrounded by cypress trees, and you realize that what is essential has no price and that what fills you cannot be bought.

But by then, it'll be too late.

Comfortably numb

You take my breath away, so I keep my head down to try and catch up with the wind. It's an old, well-known technique.
My goal is just in front of me, but it's attached to my head, so I can't reach it however far I stretch my arms.

What's important is that we all have enough to survive, just enough to end the rebellion.

Yes, there'll always be a rebellious minority, but by guaranteeing the minimum for people's survival, there won't be any revolutions.
You own eight and a half times the world's GWP, but that isn't enough for you. You have created a fairground that has gone beyond your wishes and intentions so that you are crushed and used by it for as long as it suits you, you believe you are the most crucial person in the world, but then you're thrown into the excellent waste.

Just pray that there will always be electric power.

Your richness consists of numbers on a server, a patrimony that has nothing to do with physical fatigue and honest work but that increases through algorithms and multiplies in the virtual world that exists as long as it doesn't get contaminated by the real economy.

But your piece of plastic platinum is connected to these numbers, and as long as the system works, you can buy whatever you like.

Since numbers do not refer to the "gold" reality, they can be created, multiplied, and bumped up to a place where there are no limits, as long as there is electricity and the system isn't contaminated by people's sweat.

Finance has won, money has won, and the system has defeated the middle class and has become infinitely rich, but history tells us that the greedy have come to a wrong end. And wise Solomon teaches us: *"Whoever digs a pit may fall into it; whoever breaks through a wall may be bitten by a snake"*.

We are in a system extending its control of everything and everyone in the face of the need to fight terrorism and tax evasion.
Malicious people say that this is a strategy that has been desired and carefully studied.

More people die from lawnmower accidents in the United States than terrorist attacks.

They invented the substitution of the convertibility of gold with the debt/GDP ratio based on created figures simply because they had to make sense of the relationship between currencies. They shifted the debt from people as creditors to people as debtors.

Multinational companies are on the board of the banks, and the banks are on the board of global companies. They all finance politicians, condition governments, and create and change the law to suit themselves.

So we have a system that is based on four pillars. Two of these are multinational companies and information, the third pillar is financial power, and the fourth pillar is political power, which in the end just introduces the measures decided by the main posts, finance and the multinational companies.

The role of information is to "sweeten the pill", acting with the "media cloud effect". Every week there's a piece of news that intoxicates the news bulletins, while the real needs, the real problems, the ones that it is so annoying to solve because this would go against worldwide interests, stay unresolved.

The fight against tax evasion and the tax burden is heavy on ordinary people to anaesthetise them, daze them, and simultaneously keep them busy. The places where the actual revenue and the real profits come from are ignored and protected by the laws that the multinational companies and the financial system write on an ad hoc basis.
Privileges for "them" continue to be granted. Every now and then, there is a move against someone famous to create a "mist" effect. But who knows what really happens in the end?
It's a bit like the fight against the Mafia. There are claims of having seized hundreds of millions of Euros from the Mafia, while around 10% of the GDP is laundered (Wiki money laundering), which is 200 billion Euros. The Mafia launders $5.5 billion a year.

Since "pecunia non olet", countries pretend to

introduce suffocating nooses for ordinary people. But practically make agreements with big tax evaders and organised crime. Every aspect of the "real and virtual economy" and finance is polluted.

Computers

In the '70s, I asked my brother, who was working for an American multinational company, if he'd get me onto a course to learn how to use these "new electronic devices".

By the end of the '70s early 80s, when we talked about computers in terms of work, we could only speak about IBM because they had the monopoly of the mainframes.

From the outside, IBM looked like a religious sect: only new graduates were hired, and they were sent to somewhere near Milan for their training, which was more like brainwashing than real training, after which they ended up identical, precisely the way the company wanted them, very well trained and geared to make the company profitable.

This is an apparently negative criticism of this IT giant, but it's veiled with envy because IBM was an impeccable organisation with real commercial and technological power.

When one talked about IBM computers, it was a question of an investment of millions of lire. These were mainframes with a lower computing capacity than our third-generation PCs, which took up the space of a whole room. The data processing unit had to rest on floating floors with a generator and be kept at a constant temperature.

In London, the banks swapped the magnetic tapes

every evening, so if there was a fire in one of the buildings, a copy of the data, called a backup, was always available.

I was happy when I was chosen as the pioneer of the interconnections between different types of systems. My IBM XT PC had a 5250 emulation card that let me communicate with my bank's s38 system, which at that point was no longer Comit but an Austrian bank that used the usual RPG to extract the data. This was to create a DIF (Data Interchange File) compatible with Lotus 123, the spreadsheet that, at the beginning of the 80s, had the market monopoly and was the precursor of Excel.

Some programmers at Visicalc had developed this spreadsheet that I used to set up a series of reports for banking accounting, Financial Futures, Bank of England Reports, Nostro Reconciliations, Arbitrages and Swaps. These operations took over 8 hours a day by hand, but with my IBM XT, I had to import the data with the 5250 emulation programme, convert it, press F9 to launch the calculation and wait for 35/40 minutes. I'd go for a coffee, come back and print the reports, and that was it.

Before the IBM XT PC, I'd used the Tandy, which is a system that is similar to the PC with two over 12" floppy discs (that was before the 5.25" floppy discs came into use), only with Visicalc, which was obviously very, very similar to Lotus 123.

Word processing was monopolised by Wordstar, and although the integrated Wang word processing machines were widespread, the type of Windows interface used today was produced exclusively by Apple. The programmes in the world of Microsoft MS-DOS had a command line interface, which could only be used with the keyboard, not the mouse.

I'd switch on my computer in the morning and the MS-DOS operative system, with the Lotus 123 launch command in the autoexec.bat file, automatically opened Lotus 123 for me, and I was ready to start work.

One day, for some godforsaken reason, I decided to get out of the Lotus programme, and I ended up with a black screen, a "c" at the top on the left followed by a ">" sign and the cursor, which was flashing. I panicked. What on earth was I supposed to do? Had I crashed the computer?

Nobody in the bank knew how to use a PC except for me and someone in the Dealing Room. But in another building on the other side of the road and knew less than I did.

I started calling the IBM dealer, the salesperson who used to go to the bank, but it was no good. Nobody knew what to do.

Then I had a brilliant idea: I said to myself, "switch it off !" and that's what I did. I switched it off and back on again, and as if by magic, the autoexec.bat did precisely what it was supposed to do, and the command launched the world's most famous spreadsheet.

At that time, Microsoft was only known for its MS-DOS

operating system on IBM PCs.

Later, Microsoft started offering Basic programming languages and MS Word, a dreadful word processing programme until version 5 was released; it could take up to half a day to make a table and keep it straight.

The world of databases was obviously in the hands of Ashton-Tate, with the famous Dbase, later supported by Nantucket's Clipper, which was then bought by Computer Associates. This programme made it possible to create and distribute applications, making modifications impossible without the programmer's intervention in the source files.

I stayed in London for 5 years, until 1986 and had an excellent experience using the PC. Then I came back to Rome because I was fed up with the weather, but I soon realized that I wouldn't be able to work at a bank in Rome.

First, there were only a few banks, and then none carried out similar financial activities to what I'd done in London. The Bank of Italy only authorised those transactions five years after I returned.

Then getting into a bank in Italy wasn't like in London; there were no job centres to go to where you could explain your skills and experience and then be hired and just as quickly be fired if you weren't suitable for the job.

The banking system in Rome was like a dome that you could only get into through a "back door". Nothing was clear or straightforward. There was no meritocracy or the capacity to perceive and value the staff's work. It was impossible to go to the personnel office and ask for an appointment. In Italy, Everything was complicated and confusing. And impossible to understand for anyone who was used to the English system that was perfectly clear and straightforward. With no fuss, nobody took advantage of their position and believed they were important because they had an essential role in the company. Obviously, there are frustrated people everywhere, in London too, but the need to optimise the work and the fact that the rules work limits the damage.

The missed embrace

The Emperor's stones
witness our steps that move forward slowly in the
dark
The fear of loving...
I wasn't brave enough
I didn't get through the wall
Fear won, and the flower didn't bloom
But our souls are united forever.
Time can't erase what it can't touch
Our breath will stop
The rainbow will disappear
But just as the Imperial column still dominates the
square
What has existed will never cease to exist.

McDonald's at Earl's Court, London

I walk into McDonald's, and without hesitating, I ask for a "Big Mac and French fries" in my practically non-existent English, pronouncing fries the Italian way (frees).

What usually happens in the English-speaking world is that if you don't pronounce the product's name exactly right, a somewhat unimaginative person taking your order won't understand what you want.

So a duet starts, watched by the other amused customers, where I say in a loud voice: French "frees!" and the girl taking my order states: "What ?" about 10 times in less than a minute - French "frees!", "What?" French "free!", "What?".

In the end, I look up and point at the menu on the wall, and I say in Italian, in an exasperated tone of voice: *"You got four miserable things written on that menu, and only one of them starts with French, so what is it you reckon I want ?"* PLEASE!

This interrupted our seemingly infinite verbal exchange, it surprised the girl taking the orders, and she said "French fries!" with great satisfaction, in perfect English even though she came from the far East.

By now, I was exhausted, and I said, again in Italian: *"Now you got it!"* And then in English: "Ok, yes, this, please". It was depressing to realize that I had to use

Italian to be understood. This meant that my English really was practically non-existent.

Another incident involving my limited English was one with a parrot.

This time I was at the home of a colleague of my Uncle Lucio, who worked for Time Magazine. He invited me for lunch at his house, which was in the countryside outside London and at one point, he had to go and get some wine, so I was left with his wife, who was making lunch.

She was a lovely lady whose English was tough to understand, and I only managed to understand about 20% of what she was saying.

In the beginning, I made an effort and said "sorry, sorry" every time I couldn't understand. Then I gave up, partly because I didn't want to make her think I was foolish, partly out of laziness and partly because I wanted to make a good impression and let her believe I understood. So I just nodded and smiled, with a little smile like an idiot, because I could hardly understand anything.

What little I did understand was enough to get the gist of the topic. I decided to go and stand by the French kitchen window and look at the parrot in its cage from close up.

At one point, the lady graciously gave me a clean lettuce leaf and said something that sounded like a long series of "ps fz ps fz ps fz". I was worn out by not being able to understand anything, so I boldly made it clear that I understood, and just as graciously, I thanked her, took the lettuce leaf and put it in my mouth!

It was only when the kind, polite, and discreet lady burst out laughing, with tears in her eyes, practically falling over, that I realized I'd let her see just how ignorant I was. I hadn't understood that the lettuce leaf was for the parrot, not me!

Like almost every Italian, my first job in London was as a waiter. The problem was that I couldn't take orders but could serve at the tables because I hardly spoke English, so I started working at the grand Savoy Hotel, performing at banquets. While queuing up outside a telephone booth near Hyde Park, I found this job. The guy in front of me was Italian too. He was working as a waiter (how strange!), so while we were talking he found out that I didn't have a job and that I didn't speak English and he gave me some good advice telling me about the Savoy because you didn't need to talk to English to serve at banquets, you could even be dumb (but not deaf).

I'd already occasionally worked as a waiter at my tennis club. That was before I left for the army as an officer of the Folgore Brigade. In the morning, I helped out with the tennis courts, dragging the net over the courts to make them smooth and then watering them. Then I helped at the bar and served the meals at lunchtime. In the afternoon, I helped as a tennis instructor for the SAT school; in the evening, I trained and practised. I was in the club's C and B teams and was good but not brilliant.

The only vital results for the club were when I won all the singles matches in the B series for the Nomentano team.

I was the club's favourite because my father died when I was 13. The owner took me under his wing. I didn't have to pay any fees, he found me jobs to do, and at the beginning, I was part of the tennis school, but I didn't have to pay for my lessons.

Sport kept me away from pseudo politics and the violence of the '70s in Talenti, but we were as rebellious as anyone else then. I played with Fabio, we signed up for the tournaments, and we made sure we played at the same time, but we used to get around on Fabio's Vespa and were always late, so to get there quicker, Fabio used to go straight through red lights. I was on the back of the Vespa, and I covered the number plate with my racquet.

Our group of friends at that time were reckless and irresponsible. Some of them did wheelies and tried to rest the front wheel on the back of a bus. Another time I was going to Ostia on my Vespa, and there were five other guys, one behind the other, with Vespas too, but two or three of them had the same number plate.

Anyway, at the club restaurant, I'd never served people I didn't know, in a formal way, with a tray, having to take the food with two spoons with one hand while the other hand held the tray with the food on it, like we had to at the Savoy banquets.

When they gave me the ok to start work at the grand hotel, I practised at home with some small stones that I put on a plate. I used two spoons to put little rocks onto another plate and back again onto the first one.

The serving was much more complicated than training because I was in charge of a table of about a dozen people. Everything had to be served at the right time and simultaneously as all the other waiters.
I was obviously always the slowest one, and when the dinner was over and it was time for coffee, there wasn't ever any left. I was very sorry for the guys at my table. They ended up with the coffee left over in the coffee pots, which was then poured into mine, which was empty, and if it still wasn't enough, I'd just add some hot water to make up the difference. It was undrinkable. They'd have thrown it at me in Italy, but fortunately, nobody complained. If anything, they just didn't drink it, and I couldn't understand them anyway!

One of the first times I was serving, disaster struck; there wasn't much coffee in the pot, and out of lack of experience, I didn't put my finger on the top of the pot to hold it down, so while I was serving at a table of some Germans, the top of the pot fell onto a customer's coffee cup. All the coffee spilt onto his dinner suit.

I said "sorry" a dozen times, but that wasn't enough to calm the customer. I didn't understand him because he was swearing at me in German, and I didn't even speak English, let alone German!

The head waiter came over, told me to go away, and tried to compensate for the damage.
My experience at the Savoy lasted until, thanks to my Aunt Emma and Uncle Gustavo, I started work at the Banca Commerciale. At first, I had to file the statements and know all the clients' balances. The richest one was "temporary awaiting instructions"!

A comment was made to an English colleague who always insisted on how great the British Empire was and Italy's defeat in the second World War. The power of the British in the world was an example of the student-like atmosphere at work.

One day, after yet another comment about the British Empire, I looked at my colleague, who sat opposite me and spoke good Italian. In a bored tone, I said: "If Julius Caesar hadn't come here two thousand years ago, you'd still be walking around on all fours"! Then I looked down at my work again, and my colleague was stunned. He wasn't used to that kind of Roman bluntness, and he thought I was rude.

That comment had a double positive effect because my "imperialist" colleague stopped talking to me altogether for quite a long time. Then when he did start talking to me again, it was never about "the great British Empire".

Sergio was the other Italian employee in that room, and he laughed out loud. He was from the island of Elba, he'd moved to London years earlier, and he spoke English with a Livorno dialect, so he put *"de"* everywhere.

He said, "put it there, *de*", "give that to me please, *de*", and he was the master of reconciliations and the person who taught me my job at Comit.

The five years I spent in London were fundamental for my English, which then turned out to be essential for work and everyday life, especially with the arrival of the internet and the availability of an infinite amount of helpful information.

And then, living in such close contact with English culture nourished a part of me that has always been directly influenced by Englishness because my mother and brother both had British citizenship. I'm at home in London.

I couldn't understand anything for my first three months in London. I was bombarded by unknown English words and phrases that were impossible to relate to anything I could decipher. Then I finally started to be able to speak whole sentences, but I constantly made mistakes, and I saw that my English colleagues used *"would"*, *get* and *got* a lot, but I never did. So I said to myself: "when I get stuck, I'll try to place in my speech *"would"*, *get* or *got*, so that's what I did, and my English magically became fluent!

144

The Fourth Dimension

I'm your guest until the day you tell me to go away and
you die.
Your colour will leave you, and you will seem far away.

You let me see the things of the world
and listen to every sound and every note that makes
me shiver.
You're my bridge to feelings and emotions
to pain and to joy.
You take me to places and carefully carry out the
instructions
It all works out, even if it's a lot of work and training.

You bring me close to my neighbour
To the people I love and those I hate.
It's not easy to guide you.
It's not easy to convey to you what is restless in me.
It's not easy for me to understand what is restless in
them.
It's not easy to look beyond and understand who lives
somewhere else.

You must take your time and let the sea leave lines on
your face.
People who don't know how to cry don't understand
those who fly.

Sometimes our eyes show the way to somewhere
beyond, just for a second.
I live in you. As far as I'm concerned, I'll never die
because now I exist. It's impossible not to exist, but I

145

can't say the same for you.

There'll be a time when I'll go somewhere else to *"a place none of us has been, a place that has to be believed to be seen"* (Walk on by U2).

One day I'll leave you, you'll be inhospitable, I'll explore other places, and I don't know whether I'll cry.

THE END

THE END

Giulio Credazzi's Books

100 Pagine
Distillato d'amore
Amico silenzioso
Profezie della Bibbia, i rami teneri hanno le foglie
Il Giro di Boa
Dal calendario Maya 2012 ad Armagheddon
Da Quota 33 a El Alamein
Oltre il confine della stupidità fiscale italiana
Nero su Bianco
Soluzioni di rete
Il Piano di Dio
Gli Zollari
100 Pages
Silent Friend
The Plan of God
From the Maya calendar to Harmagheddon
The turning Point

Project: Giulio Credazzi
Graphic: Caterina Bonelli
Printed indipendtly

Printed in Great Britain
by Amazon

22114404R00086